AMBER

THE BIRTH OF A QUEEN

A BLOOD PROPHECY NOVELLA

BARB JONES

This is a work of fiction. Names, characters, places, and incidents are products of the author's imagination or are used fictitiously and are not to be construed as real. Any resemblance to actual events, locations, organizations, or persons, living or dead, is entirely coincidental.

World Castle Publishing, LLC

Pensacola, Florida

Copyright © Barb Jones 2017
Paperback ISBN: 9781629896519
eBook ISBN: 9781629896526
First Edition World Castle Publishing, LLC, March 20, 2017
http://www.worldcastlepublishing.com

Licensing Notes

Cover: Steven J. Catizone
Editor: Maxine Bringenerg

By Barb Jones
Other Works:

Blood Prophecy One: Queen's Destiny
Blood Prophecy Two: Queen's Enemy
A Blood Prophecy Novella - Marcus:
Origins, A Blood Prophecy Novella
Chloe: Visions of the Futures

AUTHOR'S NOTE

First of all, thank you for entering the world of Blood Prophecy. The series is especially dear to me starting with the very first novel, "Queen's Destiny." The prophecy has been told through many different generations, through many different supernatural races, and if the races unite, peace will reign.

Amber, Chloe, Michael, and Marcus are four beautiful souls that are the essence of the series. In Amber: Birth of a Queen, learn how she was destined for greatness through her parents. I wish to thank all my fans, my street team, my friends and family for their continued support as I continue with the series. My dream is to have Blood Prophecy touch the lives of each and every reader, bringing them a sense of peace and reunification towards the good side of everything.

PROLOGUE
LINEAGE

Long before he became a father, Nikoli was destined to become the next alpha of the pack. His birthright and destiny were told by the elders of the different packs that had kept hidden from the outside world. He was a man of sixteen years, tall, with hair as black as a raven, broad shoulders, and strong arms. Nikoli was a handsome man in the pack, but he was a loner, though a capable leader. His parents, though dead now, had made him memorize the legend of his destiny. Sometimes, before he would go to sleep or before turning into a wolf, he remembered the story his father would tell him.

"The stars told of a young wolf who will mate with one from a line of dark magic and power. From their union a child will be born, but will be lost. The young wolf will yield the mark of the prophecy—a crescent moon imprinted on his shoulder. His mate will have fire colored hair. The child will be destined for the heavens, but darkness will follow her. This special one will bring forth unification and light to the werewolves of all the packs, the blood drinkers, and the seers. She will be consort to the blood drinker, have the vision of fire, and wield a scepter so strong and pure. Wolves will know her by the color of fire in her hair, her eyes of pure goodness and light, and her heart of a wolf. The child is her father's daughter, full of strength, wisdom, and power."

Nikoli would ponder this dream repeatedly over the years, keeping his faith and strength true to the legend, because he knew that he was this young wolf that the stars predicted. The pack loved him and chose to follow him when he went hunting and fishing. The younger male wolves always looked up to him, and he made sure never to disrespect the alpha.

One day, Nikoli was at home when the pack leader knocked and entered. The two men were friends and had a deep amount of respect for each other.

"Nikoli, my friend. You know the women are talking about how much you need to settle down and start a family. Our survival depends on the children we can conceive."

"Don't start with that again," Nikoli said, while chuckling at the thought of the women in the pack. He recalled how some were very beautiful and captured his attention. But he shook thoughts of them from his mind.

"What say you, lad? How about the brown haired little wolf? You know, the one they call Chehali." Arkan was similar to Nikoli in regards to personality and strength. Arkan had long blond hair, which he always kept neat and pulled back, his skin was a fair complexion, and his strength was remarkable. Nikoli always looked up to him and followed his commands. He respected his alpha.

Nikoli sat down and began to tell the story of his destiny that had been told to him many times. When he finished, Arkan stood and placed his hand on Nikoli's right shoulder. "Okay, true wolf.

We will help find your mate that the stars speak of."

***

Miriam was a young woman who had terror flashes that never let her rest peacefully. Since the Dark Man had taken her from her loving family, her nights were usually spent alone and afraid. One of her special gifts allowed her to see images, but it was hard to tell if they were from the past, present, or future. Having been taken from her family, she never had the opportunity to fully understand her gifts. Miriam was a striking young woman with red hair and soft skin. The Dark Man usually kept her in chains in her room for fear that she would escape his grasp.

In her mind she saw the image of a young, handsome man. His eyes were dark and showed a presence of courage, or at least that was what she allowed her imagination to tell her. The next flash was of another young woman. This time it seemed more sinister. The woman walked amongst fire and death. In fact, this image disturbed Miriam the most. The woman also had red hair, but she could tell that it was not her but someone close in resemblance. This woman walked with a wolf, and bodies lay burning in flames all around her feet. It sent chills down her arms and caused her to cry.

The Dark Man entered her room and commanded her to remain silent and listen.

"Child. You grow stronger each day and it is time to teach you my art. There is no light that can destroy what I bring forth. You are ready. Your heart is as black as the night, your fear calls to me, which is how I know you are ready.

I need you to channel your hatred and anger. Feel the power inside you. Do it now."

Miriam breathed deeply. She remembered how much her parents loved her. In thinking of her father, she found a strength she thought was lost. She managed to burn the chains that kept her bound. As the Dark Man approached, she set his cloak on fire and ran past him. Miriam set fire to everything around her as she managed to find her way to the front door and escaped.

Miriam was free but alone, cold, and unsure of what to do next. The image of the young man kept filling her mind, and she had to locate him. But she was young, and didn't know when or where to find him. It may take months or years, but she focused on his looks and traveled in the direction her feet took her.

Chapter One
The Birth

Nikoli looked at Miriam as she was going into labor, and his thoughts raced back in time to the day he'd met her and how they had married quickly. It was hard to believe that it had been a year since that day. Tuning out the sounds of her cries, he recalled how this beautiful woman had wandered into his pack. It made him smile as he remembered.

There he and Shulu were, gathering water and working the land, as they were a nomadic pack, even in the 1980s in Delaware. As Nikoli came closer to the pond, he saw a foot hidden

15

in the weeds. The pond was dense with weeds and made a perfect hiding place. He looked at the foot and let his eyes move up farther. In his mind he was hoping that this was not the remains of a human that one of the pack had decided to devour. His eyes continued to search, and eventually they found a beautiful face belonging to a woman who was beautiful and naked. Around her neck was a green crystal amulet. Her face had a gash on her cheek, and blood trickled from the side of her head.

Nikoli could see her chest rise and fall, though faintly...there was not much life in the woman. He bent down and picked her up, not looking at her curves or nakedness, and moved fast to bring her back to the pack.

Once she was healed they spent a lot of time together, to the point where they began to develop feelings for each other. Nikoli, very old fashioned for a werewolf, loved her *and wanted not only to consummate their relationship, but to begin a family together. He wanted her for his mate. He just knew that she was the one that was meant for him. Miriam agreed to his offer and they were wed. But after the wedding, Nikoli realized that he didn't know about her heritage, and that could pose an issue with the elders.*

He asked Miriam to tell him of her family, and what she told him surprised him and left them both with a lot of questions. He listened as Miriam told him her story.

"My parents are not all human. They are like you and your pack, but not werewolves. My family is also…shall we say, special, but in a way that might change your mind about me…."

Before she could continue to say the words that he didn't want to hear, Nikoli kissed her and reassured her. He wanted her to be his. He had chosen her. The stars had told generations of this union.

"My father is what you would call a seer. A prophet. But as such, he has special abilities that others do not. He can see into the past lives of people, supernatural or not. He can also move things with his mind, among other things. He belongs to an order, but I don't recall what order. My mother is a strong witch. She comes from a line of witches, or wiccans, or whatever they are called. But, her line of power is not at all what we would call the White Light of Power. When my parents married and formed a union, they left their families and their power behind until I was born. My birth changed things for them, and their destinies pulled them apart. I don't remember them after I turned five. I was the firstborn of a generation, and my parents hid me. Soon after I turned five, a man came for me. I didn't learn why until much later. But, I inherited my mother's fire and ran away *many years later. I've been on my own since. I've been attacked, beaten, raped, and violated by people that knew my parents, but I don't know them. In fact, you found me after I was left for dead.*

"Here's what I know about the Dark Light of Power from my mom. There is a man that the covens call the Tall Dark Man, who comes to certain witches and makes them fall under his control. Once they do, he uses their power and gives them more so that they serve him. My mother served him before I was born. My father thinks I am the child of the Dark Man, but I inherited his abilities, so I can't be. But my mother told me on the day I turned five that if I ever have my first girl child, the Dark Man will come to claim her power unless a love stronger than true helps her to rise. My father told me also that this child would rise above all and would be the queen to save the races, but her choices must be true and

worthy of her heart. It is part of a prophecy that is told from generation to generation. In fact, all the races know this prophecy. If she ever strayed from her destiny, all would be lost. When they abandoned me, as I call it, they gave me this amulet to pass down, and told me that my child must learn strength, love, and be faithful to the Blood Prophecy. I have yet to discover what all that means.

"While I lived with this Dark Man, I learned the ways of the Dark Light and could barely recall the White Light. In my dreams I would hear songs, but when I woke, there was nothing to remember.

"Nikoli, love, I don't mean to scare you, but this child…if she is the child my parents spoke of, what shall we do? I don't want to lose her, but she must be raised with her truth. But this is my family. You are my family."

Nikoli thought about his destiny and shared with her the story that had been told to him. He could sense that Miriam understood and felt the same connection. At that moment, he knew it was meant to be. All had been confirmed in that moment of time.

From that day forward, Nikoli loved her for the truth and her spirit, as it never led him away from her. But her screams brought him back to the moment. The birth. Looking at Miriam, he saw that her hair was drenched in sweat and clinging to her face, tears rolling down her cheeks as she screamed and pushed. One of the midwives from the pack was holding her legs while another let her rest against her. Both women were gently encouraging her to push.

"Push, Miriam. Push. Only a few more pushes. Bring this child forth. The pack is ready to love her. Atta girl."

Nikoli's love for her consumed him as he encouraged her to keep pushing.

21

He didn't want to lose his love or this child. Nikoli closed his eyes and prayed to the heavens that this childbirth would not take his love. When they opened once more, he could see that Miriam was tired; blood seeped through the linens, her bedding needed changing, but she had the fight in her to birth this child. He could see she was beginning to get weaker from the childbirth, but he urged her to keep going. Reaching for her hand, he closed his eyes and began to send his strength to his beloved.

Another woman entered the area and brought more clean water. Women were rushing about and whispering. Finally, a woman placed a warm mug in his hands and the smell of coffee filled his nostrils. She urged him to take a seat in the corner while the others helped his wife.

***

Miriam recalled hearing Nikoli's words of encouragement and the midwives' instructions to push harder. Sensing a power within her rising from God knew where, she gave a final push. With that final push, she slumped in the arms of the midwife and closed her eyes. Beads of sweat trickled down her cheeks, her hair was a matted mess, and she did not care that she was covered in so much blood. Through the darkness, she heard a voice.

My child. Do not fall asleep. If you do, the Dark Man will rise and seek you. He is joined to you. You are his. You must wake. Be with your child at all times, and prepare your heart to do the most painful thing in life. Take your child, your husband, and go far away. Give her a life that she is born to have, but not with you. Sense her strength and guide her till you part ways. I'm never far from you, my child. But wake now. I put a protection spell on you on the day you were born. I knew your mother's family was dark, but you…you are my child, the last of my line. Forces will come for her and try to turn her away from the light as they had done with you. I am your father, your protector. Now wake child. Wake NOW!

With a jolt, Miriam's eyes fluttered open and she heard the cry of the baby. She looked towards Nikoli and smiled. Her heart filled with love and joy as she saw him take the baby and place her in her arms. Looking down at the babe, she smiled as tears of happiness and love flowed from her eyes and onto the baby's head. She noticed that the baby didn't resemble either Miriam or Nikoli in many features. Instead, the baby took after her maternal grandfather. Miriam, as tired as she was from the labor, remembered her father fondly and saw him in the newborn. The baby was alert and seemed to possess a quiet strength within.

"Your name is Amber. Daughter of Nikoli and Miriam, granddaughter of Talios."

The baby stopped crying once Miriam called out her name. Miriam looked at the child, perplexed. The greenish eyes of the baby got her attention, but it was the red hair that stood out the most. Amber had a full head of red hair, green emerald eyes, and the cutest nose. Her eyes showed the most promise, however. It looked as if she could sense what was happening in the world around her. Miriam couldn't get over how cute her little girl was, but was saddened at the same time. How was she going to break the news to Nikoli and say goodbye to this treasure?

Amber's eyes looked straight into Miriam's eyes and the two of them instantly connected. A sense of calm rushed over Miriam, and she decided she couldn't think about the farewell that would happen soon. Instead, as she gazed at her baby, she felt a tingle stir inside her. A feeling of great power.

Looking at Nikoli, she said, "Nikoli, we must be alone with our child. Please. I need a little peace with my new family."

The midwives understood and decided to take their leave. The new family needed time alone to bond.

CHAPTER TWO
The Family

Miriam held the baby close to her bosom to nurse while she shared her thoughts with Nikoli. Well, not her thoughts only, but the words of the voice that had spoken to her. The voice of her father. She took a deep breath and began telling Nikoli as best she could about the future, and something called the Blood Prophecy. Miriam could tell that her love was listening to her, but she sensed hesitation and heartbreak from him. Knowing that she had previously told him about her family heritage, she also knew that she had failed to tell him ALL of it. Keeping the most treasured secret about herself from him meant that she was jeopardizing herself and her new daughter.

Tears came flowing again and she could hardly breathe, thinking about how much she had to tell Nikoli, and how much it would be a cross to bear for the both of them. "I am the daughter of the seer of an order. I do not recall the order or anything about them, only that I have my father's powers. Or at least I inherited them, as well as the powers from my mother. The firstborn girl child of each generation becomes the gift to the Dark Man, but I don't know who he is. I was the firstborn child of my generation, and was kept hidden. The Dark Man found me after all those years and left me for dead. Then you found me. Nikoli, we must save the baby. I'm sorry I wasn't completely honest with you about my past. But, I cannot change that. She needs protection now."

Miriam saw that he looked at her, and then he glanced around.

"Nikoli, husband. Let me tell you a little more about Talios, my father. It is important. Talios is a strong man, much like you. But he commanded not only the order but others as well. It didn't matter if you were supernatural or human, he could command you without words. Talios is strong, and I see him in Amber. She bears his features, especially the eyes. He is all knowing, just like I sense in Amber. She's going to be a quiet force to be reckoned with. Talios could see our future long before we met. Promise me, husband. Promise me we will not only save our baby girl, but we will find my father and make him answer our questions.

"The bloodline in my family is not all tainted. In fact, our bloodline is a mixture of both pure light and dark light. We know not how far it goes back, but legend tells us that it goes back to the start of the world. Regardless, in my blood light and dark flow, but the world has been waiting for a special one to come. Should our daughter be this special one, her blood will have to choose the path of either light or dark. Do you understand?"

***

Nikoli heard every word and all he could do was nod in agreement. Wanting to hold his baby daughter, he reached out to take her from her mother's arms. The baby's green eyes looked up at him and the cutest sounds came from her. His heart was filled with pride and love as he gazed at her. His eyes met hers, and before he could gently speak to her, a vision was imprinted in his mind.

He saw the cutest red headed child looking at a different couple. The couple wasn't him and Miriam, but another older couple. They took the little girl's hand and walked out of a building together. Around her neck was Miriam's amulet.

The image faded from his mind and his heart felt relief. He knew Miriam was right. The babe needed protection, but he wanted time with his new child. Her little chubby arm flailed towards him, and with his right index finger he reached out to touch her little fingers. Baby Amber smiled at him and he felt his heart break. Handing her back to Miriam, Nikoli went to think about what to do.

While he was gone, the sky darkened and the rain began to pour. He tightened up his coat and began to walk a little faster towards the community. Seeing some of the pack members gathered around a fire pit, he couldn't wait to share with them the news of the birth till he remembered what Miriam had said. Turning up his collar, Nikoli turned around and went back to his little family's camp.

As he was walking, a soft voice—a little girl's voice, in fact—called to him.

Don't be afraid. I am small but I know my path. I was born for a reason, a reason that the world will not understand. My power is strong and I will be queen. Father, do not fear. My life will prepare me for the means to the end.

With that, as Nikoli entered their camp, the babe closed her eyes and went to sleep against her mother's breast. Nikoli beamed at his family with pride and contentment, but deep down he dreaded the ultimate sacrifice that would be made to protect his daughter. Looking at Miriam, he could only imagine what she could be thinking or feeling, given her latest news.

"Love, we must prepare our daughter for the fate that has fallen. You are right. But before we release her into the world to protect her, let's spend time together as a family. What say you, my sweetheart?"

Miriam replied, "Nikoli, of course. Come sit with us."

***

Amber was in a light sleep, nestled against her mother's breast. She may have just been born, but she was a wise newborn with senses intact and developed more than her parents could imagine. She knew the destiny that was bestowed upon her as well as her upcoming fate, but she remained silent.

After all, she was just a newborn babe.

Her mind was working with the voices in her head. Voices she had heard for thousands of years, and she knew them intimately. She listened as they told her not to be afraid and that her parents would always love her. Cooing and making other various baby noises only caused her mother, Miriam, to hold her more closely than she was already.

Amber decided to make a connection once more with her father. She knew she could trust him. With her eyes still closed, she let her mind reach out to Nikoli. Her mind searched and finally connected with his, but she didn't let him know she had entered his mind. Searching through his thoughts, Amber was able to find a certain one. She wanted to know more about the parents that she would soon lose. Images of her mother and father filled her mind.

She saw her father carrying her mother, naked, from a pond to the village. His hand moved her hair away so that he could see her face. Amber may not have heard the words he spoke to her, but she could see the love he had for her mother in that memory. Trying hard not to scare her father, she whispered her thoughts to him once more.

Father. Do not be afraid. What will come, will come. Open your mind to me so that I can see the history of our family, so that my future will hold true. Know that I understand the wolves and can wolfspeak. You may not know why, but I assure you, Father, I am true. Close your eyes and let me speak to you. Feel my power. Feel my strength. I am the one the world has been waiting for. The one the wolves speak of in their legends.

***

He was stirred from his thoughts by

this tiny voice. Nikoli did as requested by his cute princess. Images filled the darkness in his mind, and what he saw was a miracle. Wolves, vampires, witches, other races bowing to a beautiful red-headed woman surrounded by flames and a light, and around her neck was an amulet. At her side was a child, and on the other, a man. The man seemed strong, and he held her hand. Could this woman be his sweet girl? The images were replaced with images of a battle between the races, bloodshed, and more violence. Then, the final image was of Miriam. Not her, but her tombstone that read, "Beloved Mother, Loving Wife, and More."

Shaking his head to free his mind of these images, Nikoli managed to get one of his pounding headaches. Struggling to reach his cottage, he called out to Miriam, who in turn helped him. Holding his sweet girl, he looked down at the tiny face and fingers, and decided that his family must be together before anything changed their circumstances.

"Miriam. Love. We can't abandon our Amber just yet. We must imprint on her. There must be an honorable wolf in the pack that is destined to be her mate. Let's give it some time."

"Okay, Nikoli. But the imprint to a newborn seems dangerous. I don't understand what you mean by imprint. Look at her coo. She's a sweet little thing."

"Imprinting is when one wolf feels so strongly for another that he would do anything for her. It's more than love, more than physical attraction. He would lay down his life for her, give her anything she needs, protect her. Do you understand, love? Well, when Amber is older and a young woman, the two will become lifemates. She will bear his children and keep the pack alive even if she is not with us. He will be with her. It's more than a lifebond…it's a lovebond. It's kind of magical.

"So before we give her up to save her, we must imprint on her or die trying, so that her future — a future she showed me — will come to pass."

Miriam started to cry.

***

Miriam couldn't stop crying. Before falling in love with Nikoli, she had been left to die and knew no kindness. Nikoli had shown her kindness and brought her back to life. Looking down at her new baby girl, Miriam knew that her family history was going to catch up with her sooner at later. But, had bearing a werewolf's child brought much more trouble than she had imagined? What about what the baby showed Nikoli? Why didn't Baby Amber communicate with her?

The more she thought about this, the more tears she shed. The baby looked up at her and smiled. Miriam felt like Baby Amber could read her mind, and she was no more than a few hours old. Looking down at the sweet girl, Miriam could feel thoughts in her head. She shook her head in confusion. She again looked into the eyes of Baby Amber.

Mother, Mother. You are scared about something you are not yet ready to comprehend. I am your baby. I am also going to be queen. But through your bloodline, I am more than that. The Dark Man haunts you, and he is coming.

"Sweet little Amber."

Miriam started to sing a soft song to Amber, and listened to her coo as she sang the song. Memories of the Dark Man claiming her came back and haunted her core. She recalled the day that the Dark Man had come and taken her from her mother's arms. It was the last day she saw her parents, and her father had been practically powerless against him. In fact, that was the day that he'd killed both of them, and she feared that the same would happen to her and Nikoli if the Dark Man learned about the sweet baby girl.

Hopefully, imprinting on the child would help her in life if the Dark Man were to come for her.

Chapter Three
Imprint

Days passed and Amber continued to be aware of everything around her and her parents. Her green eyes soaked up the world and the pack celebrated her birth. It had been lifetimes since the pack welcomed a special child into their circle. Amber found it easier to speak to her father than her mother, because for some reason, her mother kept holding something back that prevented her from revealing the destiny and truth that she was born into. She could feel it.

She was snuggled in a baby blanket

alone in her bassinet. Her mother had just fed and burped her and placed her down to sleep. Amber didn't want to sleep. Inside she knew that babies slept a lot, but she didn't need to. Most times she only pretended to because her mother and father kept soothing her to sleep. Her mind was racing with the things she must learn to do while waiting for this tiny body to grow.

Being only a few days old, Amber was already a healthy little thing. She nursed like she was six months old and her appetite never ceased. Her memories of the past and the images of the future caused her to make cooing noises. She reached her mind out, searching for her father. Though she was a newborn, her powers were unimaginably strong. In fact, Amber had known about her abilities while she was in her mother's womb.

Memories of a maternal grandfather calmed her soul. She knew that Talios was the strongest warlock in the order, but not strong enough to defeat the Dark Man. Amber felt the power in her grow, and though just a tiny babe, she was all knowing, all seeing, and all powerful. This power was so strong that when Amber felt the tiniest amount of pain, she cried. It wasn't a regular type of pain. Amber knew that the power she had within was too much for the little body she had. In time it would be controllable, but for right now, it was a lot to endure. The tiny baby knew how to subdue the pain with a powerful enchantment that was only from her memories.

Closing her green eyes once more, images of the past queens flowed through her mind. Strength, formidability, power, and fierce intelligence all claimed her soul in the end. She then sent a picture of a young man to her mother…the young man she knew to be part of her future. Amber smiled as she hoped her mother would know what to do. Her destiny was calling to her and she felt the pull.

One of the images that Amber saw was of a queen being consumed by fire. She saw another man with her, and wolves. For an infant, Amber knew what these things were because she was an old soul within the body of the infant. She began to cry and as she did, her mother came to comfort her. The feeling of being held was soothing and the horrible image disappeared.

***

Nikoli and Miriam walked among the various pack members, searching for the young man that had entered the village around the same time that Nikoli found Miriam. Soon, Nikoli returned home with the baby, but she continued on. She felt that something was bothering Nikoli and that he needed space. Eventually Miriam spotted the man, and she walked a little faster to reach him.

"Malakai? Can you please speak to Nikoli and me about an urgent personal matter?"

Malakai turned around and Miriam motioned for him to follow her. He nodded and was walking behind her, trying to match pace but not to be disrespectful by walking next to her. Rules of the pack dictated that mates walked next to each other, and non-mates walk behind.

They entered and found that Nikoli had his back to them. Miriam thought that he looked lost in thought, so she cleared her throat to get his attention. It worked, because Nikoli turned around and hugged her. Then he grasped Malakai's hand in a very firm handshake.

"Malakai, good of you to meet us like this. I know you must be wondering why. Please come and sit."

"I will fix some coffee for the three of us." Miriam began to prepare the coffee and listened for the baby.

***

Malakai took the cup that was offered and began to drink from it. He was perplexed as to why he was there, but he'd always been the kind of person who liked intrigue and mystery. His dark hair was pulled back into a ponytail, the way he always wore it, and he never went anywhere without his shades. Malakai had been welcomed into the pack like family, and no one questioned where he came from. He had the scent of an alpha, and his presence seemed to command obedience from all wolves, but he never once used that gift against his new family. Instead, he followed the alpha of this pack and led by example. By doing so, the alpha gave him the utmost respect and asked him to be his second. No one objected to this change.

Waiting for someone to tell him what was going on was a test of patience, but he remained calm. Suddenly, Nikoli interrupted his thoughts by bringing the baby forward. The baby was unwrapped from her swaddling so that her face could be seen. Gently she was placed in his arms, and Malakai had no choice but to look at her.

The baby cooed and Malakai looked into her eyes. For a tiny moment, he felt an unspeakable pull that drew him to her. Their eyes connected and the baby smiled. Malakai could not form the words he was thinking, and remained enraptured by the smile. The next thing he knew, he felt a sense of peace come over him as he moved his finger to touch hers.

Images were appearing in his mind, and he couldn't fathom where they were coming from. But in his heart, somehow he knew the answer, though he didn't understand why. He felt a connection to her, but she was just a baby. The way he'd heard it through his family was that each had to be at least seven years of age. It was unheard of for such a connection with a baby.

"Nikoli, I feel strange. I think…I think I should leave. Perhaps we can talk later about whatever it is you wanted to see me about?"

"No, Malakai. Please stay. Nikoli will

explain things to you. Have another cup of coffee?" asked Miriam.

The baby started to cry and Malakai's instinct kicked in. He began to rock her and looked at her. The first words out of his mouth to her were, "Shhh, Princess. You are bound to me. I am bound to you. I serve no other but you."

He couldn't stop the words from being spoken, but as he said them, the skies turned from blue to black and a lightning flash pierced the sky.

***

Amber sensed his thoughts and gave a little coo. She couldn't speak words, being a baby, but she could send images to communicate, which she did for Malakai. It was an image of the past; a woman with fangs surrounded by wolves, and a man holding a wolf in particular. The wolf was broken and in chains while the

49

woman cried. She sent another image of a red headed young woman and Malakai, holding hands amongst the wolves and vampires.

The baby hoped that the young man that spoke the words could make sense of the pictures, because this was her past and her future. Her only hope was that mortal time would move faster so that she could speak one day. But for now, she felt his imprint on her, and it was now her turn.

***

Nikoli interrupted things by slapping Malakai on his shoulder.

"It seems you have already done what we needed. We needed to find someone in the pack to imprint on our daughter. We must send her away, for her future is already spoken of and her journey is to begin. But, I will tell you what we know.

Miriam—take the baby please."

Nikoli breathed deeply and hung his head low. It broke his heart to tell the truth, as he had just learned it himself, so it was still so new and emotional for him.

"The baby is a special gift. She has a past, present, and future that is tied to the prophecy that we tell stories of. You know how our race was once inflicted with savagery by the vampires? Ah yes, good that you do. Well, this child is the one they speak of. Not only does she carry the lineage of the wolf, but she also possesses the power of the witches. It is almost like she is half wolf, half witch. But, she sent me images. She is a strong one. She must be sent away before a wicked man comes for her. It is her destiny to remain good, but she is just an infant right now. We needed her to imprint on someone, if possible, to protect her.

"Malakai, did she mark you? By your words it seems that she has, but only you can answer if she marked you."

Malakai nodded in silence. "I believe I was marked. I couldn't control what I was saying. How do I tell?"

Nikoli smiled gently and said, "Remove your shirt."

Malakai removed his shirt and Nikoli could see his tight abs, strong shoulders, and definitely the one thing that signified the connection. Malakai was marked, and as Nikoli's finger touched the marking, it began to glow red and Malakai looked to be in pain as his breathing became short. Nikoli pulled back his finger and called for Miriam to bring the baby.

Holding the baby so that she could see the imprint, Nikoli held her little finger to touch the marking and Malakai breathed easier. The marking gave a final glow and disappeared. Looking at the baby, both men were puzzled. Nikoli sat back down while holding the baby in his arms.

"She is more than what she seems. Imprints are nothing like this. Malakai, are you all right?"

Malakai nodded and began to speak.

"Sit, Nikoli. Sit, Miriam. It is time I tell you my version of the prophecy from my pack."

CHAPTER FOUR
LEGENDS

"Our version of the prophecy is more like a legend or story that is told, though no one knows the truth behind it. It is similar to yours but with one exception. She is protected, but her life is not ordinary. We say that she is the savior of the wolves by transforming into a wolf once she chooses to save them. She is constantly reborn to find her wolf twin, and once she merges, the world will be saved," Malakai said.

Both Miriam and Nikoli looked at each other and then back at him.

"Nikoli, we must save her. It seems that all our fates are tied to our baby and the power she holds."

Malakai stood once more, still wearing no shirt, and reached for Amber. It was as if the baby sensed him and she started to cry. Malakai was still in pain from the marking, but the baby was crying. Could she feel his pain? He couldn't quite tell.

Holding her closer to the marking, he touched her cheek and her green eyes looked at him with wonder. The next thing he knew the marking was gone and so was the pain. Malakai closed his eyes and maintained his sense of balance since he was holding Amber. He let his mind reach hers, using a technique he remembered from his father. Slowly it began to feel like tentacles reaching into her mind. He couldn't sense anyone else but him and Amber, as if they were the only two in the world. Finally, they were connected.

Sweet Mother of—

Calm yourself, Alpha. It is only me, the babe that you hold. But I am older than my body. I am the true queen. The one that everyone whispers about.

But you are just a babe. A newborn. Half wolf, it seems. I am Malakai, faithful and true alpha of my pack. Not of this pack, but an older pack.

You are my chosen. I knew the images I would send to my mother and father would work. There is no time. You must hear and listen to what I share with you now.

In a time where races were not equal, your kind were once slaves to my kind, as well as to others. It's been a long battle between the two major foes. My oldest self did not approve of such a fate, and I befriended one particular wolf. His name was Giorgos. He's been lost to me until I find him again. I feel him…he just has not been awakened yet. We were cursed to be separated because no wolves were to be slaves to another again.

My oldest self decided to rid the world of such atrocious ideas and sought out unification. The king could not bear the fact that I did not love him. In fact, he burned and cursed me so that I would not be able to love another. However, through the ages I have become my true self again and again, and through love, I managed to endure the curse. The king, I learned through later pieces of me, became cursed through his choosing. He sends the blood drinkers and other wretched creatures after each version of me, and each time I die, never having fulfilled the prophecy. But I am stronger with each life, and more adept to the prophecy than the last. The blood in this body is the key to the end of the prophecy. It is the key to my failure as queen.

Do you accept the choice I made for you? The burden for you to carry? As I grow, I will not allow one side of me to remember you until it is time. When I remember and unite with you, when my path is set, I will merge the two halves of me into one. Then and only then will I be true. The same holds true for the king. He must merge part of him with his true self in order to succeed. If you accept, you will eventually find what you seek, friend.

Malakai smiled at the thoughts that were shared with him. Still remaining silent, he spoke to the baby with his thoughts.

Yes, child. I accept and will do what you ask of me. If I find your lost friend, I will bring him to you.

Stay with me and my parents. There will be a day when we must part. But for now, I sense the others are coming for me. My truth is in the family line. I am of the order and of the pack.

The baby smiled earnestly at Malakai with her green eyes. He looked at her and his face remained soft.

"I will stay with you, Nikoli, with your family. The baby and I are connected, but not 'imprinted' as you call it. It seems we are more than that, and I am her sworn protector."

With that said, Malakai handed the baby back to them and took his leave. The parents looked more perplexed than ever, but Malakai reminded them that he would return.

***

Miriam held the baby and looked deeply into her eyes. The more she remembered of her past life, the more she could feel her power awakening. She'd stopped using her power because she feared the Dark Man and his wrath. She knew that the power she possessed was a result of the Good Light and the Dark Light. The challenge was which power would be her ultimate sacrifice?

She closed her eyes and tried to find a way to communicate with the little princess. After minutes of struggling, she took a deep breath, relaxed her mind, and started once more.

This time it worked. In Amber's little mind, Miriam could see images of people, wolves, and other supernatural things. All the women in the little girl's mind had a common trait...they all had green eyes. And finally, she saw it...an opening. A way to talk to her little girl. It started with an image of her nursing Amber, and it looked like she was singing to her.

Miriam thought of images to send to

Amber. First was an image of her and Nikoli when they first met. She showed Amber how much Nikoli loved her and how happy they both were while the baby was in the womb. Amber responded by showing her more images. Images of people unknown to Miriam, but they all had the green eyes.

A mother's love breaks through all obstacles, and Miriam kept showing Amber how much she was loved by her parents. The final image was the image of the path that the parents must take. But instead of tears, Miriam was filled with warmth and love by the image that Amber sent back. It was an image of her and Malakai in the future. Miriam held on to her baby tighter, hoping to send as much love as she could muster to Amber.

***

Nikoli found his beloved and their

daughter in a loving tender moment. He did not wish to disturb them, but in his mind, an image appeared of vampires headed towards the pack. The vampire leader—he assumed this because he was in front—appeared to be a savage. Blood was dripping down the corners of his mouth, and his fellow vampires were just as evil looking. The next image was that of Amber being taken away, but she did not appear to be a newborn. She had grown some but not a lot, for she was still a baby. Another image appeared in which these vampires were staking his daughter, but she was not a vampire. They were killing her!

He screamed, interrupting the peaceful moment between his loves. Miriam rushed towards him, asking, "Dear husband, what is the matter? Can't you see Amber and I are just fine?"

"No, my love, we aren't. The baby. They are coming, but I don't know when. She sent me visions of such a future. We must prepare and work with Malakai on the plan of action. The time is now! We must begin to save her. She must live even if we sacrifice ourselves. As I understand her in my limited ways, she has a destiny so great that everything must be done to ensure her life and safety. I will speak to Malakai and the elders."

***

The elders listened as Nikoli told them about the special abilities of his daughter with Malakai standing next to him. The elders very rarely came out into the community, but in important matters, they did. They were the strongest, wisest, and oldest of the werewolves. The leader of the elders, Dishku, spoke first.

"Legends tell the story of a great

woman, but no one knows where she started from. She is so great that the leaders of all the different races, except the full humans, are afraid of her. They say that she has a connection to each race through blood or other ties, but her destiny lies greater than what we know. This is how it is supposed to have started out. Sit, everyone, and listen.

"Long before we walked the earth, a Great One existed; some call him God, Father, Creator, and other names. He is the creator of all, and he made not only man but the wolves, vampires, and more. The Dark One is the brother of the Great One. The two had a falling out based on the world. The Great One loved the light and everything in it, while the Dark One did not like living under the soil.

"One day, the Dark One captured and tempted some of the creations by transforming them into hideous monsters, known as demons. Demons were sent to destroy the creations of the world and bring forth chaos, destruction, and evil. The Great One fought the Dark One with all he could, but it wasn't enough. Through their war, the world was separated even more. Then, the Great One created a woman. But this was no ordinary woman. She was perfect in every way, and carried traces of all his creations in one being. She was part human, part wolf, part vampire, part witch, and more.

"This woman, a gentle creature, proved to be the Great One's greatest attempt in defeating the Dark One. He created her in a divine image of unification, purification, and goodness. The king and the queen met, fell in love, and became betrothed. This king and queen are who people refer to as the first man and first woman of creation, and through them, all races are created. However, the Dark One is a trickster, and began his manipulation on the man. The Dark One knew that the man would one day turn, and it was just a matter of planting the seeds in his mind before that happened. He filled his head with thoughts that the other races, like ours, were to be nothing more than servants to their race. We were dogs and lived like slaves. She was beautiful, sweet, and our savior. The king didn't know that she was sent from the Great One to help him see the error of his ways. But it didn't happen that way. Instead, he burned her with flames and cursed her to a life of rebirth.

"The legend continues that until she meets the ones that will unite all, she will continue to be reborn. When she finds her pack, then she will be crowned and the battle between all will rage. If her blood sheds into a chalice, the Dark One will prevail. The end of the races will come with the fall of the Great One. But, the war hasn't been fought yet, and the brothers are preparing for this over time.

"As time moves forward, this queen is constantly reborn and destined to find her army of friends to save the races. The legend continues to say that when she is finally reunited with her army, a red moon will appear. That is when the battle will begin. Alas, that is the end of the legend as we know it."

Nikoli and Malakai looked at each other, and Nikoli cleared his throat.

"Great elders, my wife just had a baby. A girl. The naming ceremony has not happened yet, but I'm afraid the queen has been reborn, because she communicates with images and I've seen them coming for her."

Dishku said, "Bring the child to us. Now."

It wasn't a request but an order. Nikoli left immediately and returned with the baby.

Handing over his precious girl to the elder, Nikoli held onto Malakai's shoulder for comfort during this time. Dishku looked at her and smiled. He spoke in the old wolf tongue as part of the ritual.

"Child, you are the one. The wolf warrior, the human, the witch, the blooddrinker. Through you, the Great One lives. Show me who you are, child."

***

Amber looked at the elder through her baby eyes. She realized that her body may belong to an infant, but her memories, her soul, her essence, belonged to Illyris and others who had been born before her. Through space and time, her soul grew in power in order to find the perfect body, the perfect "host" in which the prophecy would be fulfilled. She decided to make that sweet cooing sound that the people seemed to love.

Closing her baby eyes and opening them once more, she was able to turn them from green to a yellow color. The man that she looked at narrowed his eyes in wonderment and he smiled.

"Yes, babe, show me who you are. It's all right, little one. You are safe amongst friends. We are the wolves. The protectors of the prophecy, as we like to think."

Once more, Amber closed her eyes and opened them once more. She started to send images of Illyris, the wolves, and the more recent images of the vampires that were coming for her. She sent images of fire, death, a gold chalice, and what would be the older image of her future self, should she live. While sending images to the great man, she pulled his memories and saw them in her mind.

Dishku remained focused on her for some reason. He didn't look away but tears rolled down his cheeks. Amber did the one thing she knew would help... she opened her baby mouth and let out a wail. The man rocked her to soothe her, so she stopped. She couldn't bear to see him cry when she had more to show him.

Amber sent more images to him. This time she showed him that Nikoli, Malakai, and Miriam were lifeless on the ground with vampires all around. Dishku was on all fours with a collar bound to his neck. The next image was of Malakai and Nikoli taking her to a place away from the camp, hopefully in time. The choice Dishku would make would result in one of the two images. With all her strength, she showed him the image of herself, a woman, with Malakai and other vampires and wolves in a peaceful life. Then she showed him the image of the chalice. Amber had the ability to recall past lives and future possibilities in images to show people. However, newborns lost this gift after the first few months of life. It was the nature of rebirth.

***

Dishku remained vigilant and eager for the images; however, he knew what they meant. It was for this special child's life that she must depart from the place of her birth. He ordered Malakai, Nikoli, and Miriam to take the child and save her. Not only did her life depend on it, but the lives of countless others. As he stared into their faces, his face softened.

"Parents of special children have a place of honor and sacred duty according to our laws. Do you know who your child is?"

Miriam spoke first. "No, Elder Dishku. I only know she has special abilities. She sends images in our minds to communicate."

Nikoli and Malakai shook their head in agreement.

"Your child is not a child. She may be a baby physically, but her soul is thousands of years old. This is the child that we have been waiting for. She is the rebirth of our beloved queen and friend to the wolves. Illyris lives in this child. She is Illyris and Illyris is her. She will have the characteristics of the races according to the Wolf Prophecy. The baby must be saved before the vampires come here to kill her. Take her, leave now with the protection of the pack. When you return, do not come here. Instead, go to the home of our eagle friends. You know the place. Do not speak of where you are headed, for the vampires will know. Travel safe and save the child. Her time has not yet come to die. She will not die on our watch.

"Go, go now. May the winds of our fathers give you speed for your flight."

Looking once more at the precious child, he blessed her with the feather from his fur and wished her a safe journey and a safe life.

CHAPTER FIVE
WINDS

The two men set out on their journey with haste. The baby was bundled tightly and carried across the front like a little package. It was easier than holding her and walking over the hills, barren paths, and other places before reaching the city. During the journey, Malakai and Nikoli talked more and more about the prophecy and the imprinting that was done.

Malakai and Nikoli had never experienced the imprinting before, and since that connection between Amber and Malakai had been made, they talked about it but were unsure of how it was supposed to feel. Malakai tried to form the right words about the feeling, but struggled in describing it. He did the best he could, though.

"Nikoli, I swear on my family's lineage, I will protect your daughter even at the cost of my life. But I can feel what she feels. Right now, she is cold."

Upon hearing that, Nikoli wrapped her up tighter. He stroked her little cheek, kissed his fingers, and placed them on her cheek. Malakai continued talking.

"I'm not sure how it is supposed to be, but I feel stronger with her near me. I know she feels the same. It's not a romantic love, Nikoli, but more like a protection kind of love. I hope that makes sense, because I'm one confused man."

Nikoli laughed and slapped the other

man on the back. "Yes, I understand. You won't be marrying my infant any time soon."

The two men laughed and the baby started to coo.

***

As the group continued their journey, the wind began to pick up. Nikoli wondered if they needed to make camp. One thing for certain was that they should avoid the main roads and anything else that would make them easy targets to spot. Finding a clearing near a tree and a stream, they began to set up camp and build a fire. Malakai took the baby and began to feed her some milk.

Nikoli hustled in preparing the camp, and almost tripped over Malakai and the baby. The wind was blowing fiercely that evening, and it was getting colder. Turning his collar up around his neck, he then cupped his hands and blew the warm air onto his fingertips. Suddenly remembering he had gloves in his pack, he put them on.

Heading towards the stream, he decided to try his luck at catching dinner. Before Nikoli waded into the water, he looked to the sky and said a prayer of thanks. Part of the wolf nature was to acknowledge the circle of life and give thanks. Upon finishing, the heavens opened up and a strong gust of wind came across the land. Closing his eyes, he tried to sense what the heavens were telling him. He also sensed whispers in his ears, but opening his eyes revealed nothing. His eyes closed once more, allowing him to really focus. Then he heard it again.

Take the child before the dawn breaks. Rest tonight; food will sustain you and your party. She must live, but stay away from the west. Head north, no one will find her there. We will guide you. Follow the trail of the leaves. The leaves will show you the path of your journey.

As he opened his eyes, fish were lying at the edge of the water, dead, ready to be cleaned and cooked. Nikoli looked up to the heavens and said a quiet prayer of gratitude, and vowed that he would follow the leaves to save his daughter.

When he returned to the campsite, he found Amber asleep on a pile of blankets and Malakai tending to the fire. Both men cleaned the fish and prepared the evening meal.

As they sat in silence eating, Nikoli heard a rumbling in the bushes from behind. Both reached behind their backsides and gripped the edges of the knives they kept hidden in their pants.

One hand told Malakai to take the baby and hide her, and the other gripped the knife even harder. The rustling became stronger, and all of a sudden the cry of the baby broke the silence.

The noise became louder till Nikoli made out the image of Miriam. "Dammit, woman, what are you doing here? We could've harmed you."

"I'm…I'm so sorry, husband. I missed her so much, and I saw images of the three of you so I had to come." Hanging her head down in shame, she began to cry.

Nikoli hated to see his love cry. He moved closer to her and held her. Gently, he said, "Go to her. Care for our baby."

***

Amber felt incredible now that Miriam held her to her bosom. She had a sense of peace and tranquility flowing over her, knowing that her world was together in this moment. But even though she was so young, Illyris was tugging at her mind with the images of wolves and flames. Her infant body became tense and she cried. It alerted her mother to soothe her again, but the images did not stop.

Instinctively, Amber sent images of the wolves and flames to her mother. Miriam's mind opened to her, and she continued to send other images as well; a blood moon, other creatures, and a red haired woman. She saw her mother smile and Amber went to sleep. Though the images scared her, she wanted Miriam to know that her life would be saved if Nikoli continued the journey.

BARB JONES

CHAPTER SIX
JOURNEY'S END

Nikoli encouraged the party to rest as much as they could after the excitement died down. He planned to start travelling again before daylight. The group had agreed that this was the best idea. The night wind calmed down, and he periodically checked on Amber and Miriam. It was best to give them privacy, because before too long, his love would have to give up their child, and even though he would too, he understood it was much harder for a mother to do.

Lovingly he put another blanket over

the two girls in his life. He wished that things would be different. Feeling that he was too restless, he walked towards the stream once more. Hoping to seek answers to what awaited them or a way to find peace for all involved, he sat down at the bank and waited. Nothing happened.

Suddenly, he saw an image. It was not human or a wolf, but something other… not exactly surreal, but something close to it. Nikoli could see through the image but it didn't look like it would harm him, so he approached it silently. Reaching his hand out, he tried to touch it. His fingers passed through what would have been his clothing. Pulling his hand back, beads of sweat began to drip down his forehead and he started to tremble. This was unlike anything else he had seen. The next thing he knew, the image motioned for him to look into the water.

The water stopped moving…it was as still as it could be. A vampire's face was shown in the water, drinking from a cup of some sort. Nikoli couldn't make out many of the details about the cup, but a demon appeared next to the vampire and took his turn drinking from the cup, then passed it around to other fuzzy images. Next, he saw a lifeless body in the water…a woman with red hair.

He looked back to the image, which pointed to the west and shook his head. Another sign to travel north. The image looked to the night sky and nodded once. A wind began to blow and howl.

Nikoli didn't like the feeling he was getting. He looked one final time at the image and said, "I am taking them now. Tired or not, we are leaving this place. I vow to protect my daughter and save her. If the gods tell me to go north, then north is where I will go. We will leave now."

Running back to the camp, he woke up Miriam and Malakai. The three packed as quickly as they could and Miriam gathered up the baby. In the dark of the night, they travelled north.

***

Malakai took the rear, keeping Miriam in the middle with the baby. He began to smell something in the air and called out.

"Nikoli, we got company. Take them and I will stay behind. I will find you."

Transforming into a wolf, Malakai was a magnificent creature. Hunched down on all fours, he began sniffing the ground for a scent and picked it up. His eyes narrowed and he bared his teeth. Saliva started dripping down as his nostrils flared. In all reality, he was a wolf ready to attack.

He continued to smell the intruder. It was a damp, foul smell…the eerie smell of death. Then he appeared, the intruder himself. Malakai howled to the sky, as if signaling for another sign to help him with this intruder. There he stood, six feet tall, dark and eerily dressed in a coat and hat. His eyes glowed yellow and his right hand reached out, finger crooked, and motioned for the wolf to come. Instead, the wolf responded with a snarl.

Circling the area while moving closer, the wolf paced himself. In his mind he pictured Amber, the cutest little baby, smiling at him. Her eyes showed the impressions of an older soul, strong and courageous. This gave him the strength to attack the intruder. Leaping into the air, he opened his mouth, stretched out his hind legs, and aimed for the man's arm. Teeth stabbed into the skin, even though the arms tried to block the attack. Holding onto the arm, the wolf put more pressure into the bite, tearing at the flesh of the intruder.

"*Câine, de control şi de randament.*" (Translated: Dog, control and yield).

The wolf understood what was said and released his bite. He heeled at the tone and stared at the stranger.

"*Modifica ţi alte auto şi ascultă-mă. Voi vorbi în limba ta apoi.*" (Translated: Change to your other self and I will speak in your tongue.)

Malakai stood naked in front of the stranger, not ashamed, but bold. It was not in his nature to show fear.

"Wolf man, I am not your enemy. Listen closely. I am one of the guardians of the prophecy. Neither you, the father, nor the mother realize the power of the girl child. She is the one we have been waiting for. Her bloodline is pure in the fact that she is descended from humans, witches, and wolves. Her life is not yet over, but will be if you don't hurry. The sky will protect you, but the ground will be twisted. It will try to destroy your goal. You must get to the city, where she can be protected. You must deliver her only to the building with the angel on the doorframe. No other place. That is a sacred building for the child's protection. Hurry."

"Whoa. What or who are you? I'm not going to take orders from a complete stranger, let alone an ass."

"You are one that was chosen, yet you do not see it. The baby. She chose you. Didn't she?"

Malakai nodded, still unsure of the

stranger.

"Young wolf, you are part of the prophecy. She chose you to protect her. There are forces outside the prophecy that seek to protect her so that she can fulfill her destiny. Guard her through her life. But there will be obstacles on this journey that will make the mother falter and change her mind. You must be the courage that this family needs. Stay to the north because the vampires are coming towards you now. They are not followers of the prophecy. They have speed, but you have cunning. Use it to save the child."

Before Malakai could say another word, the stranger vanished.

Sensing the urgency, Malakai changed back to wolf form and ran to catch up with the family.

***

Nikoli and Miriam were still walking when he heard Malakai running and panting. Turning around, he stood facing Malakai. Reaching into his bag, he gave the young man a fresh set of clothing. "Tell me what you found as we walk. Miriam, give him some water."

The baby was still asleep but smiled. Nikoli loved his baby, but was determined to hear what Malakai had to say.

"Nikoli, we must hurry. They are coming towards us. The man was a stranger, but seemed more like a friend to the baby. It was strange. I could see through him, but he spoke like you and me. At first I thought I was imagining things. The important part of his message is that we must deliver her to a building with an angel, no other place. We have to make haste now. They will find us. But we must stay strong and be sure of this. If we fail, the prophecy will fail. The baby, the sweet baby, will die."

"Yes, we will hurry. We will follow you and the stranger's advice. Show us the way. Miriam, give me the baby so that you can walk faster. Follow and stay close."

Nikoli swaddled the baby and slung her in the carrier he made that hung across his chest. The group pushed on with Malakai leading in confidence, until the first obstacle stopped them.

A large tree blocked the path that they were on. Normally it wouldn't be a problem to go around such a tree, but this was different. A swarm of deadly snakes was all around the ground and tree, not slithering, but waiting for the group to make a move so they could strike. Miriam hated snakes. Nikoli and Malakai stopped dead in their tracks and motioned for Miriam to stay back. The baby started to squirm despite Nikoli's attempts at trying to keep her calm.

The biggest snake started to move now, its eyes a deep black. Nikoli thought he heard it say something, but knew snakes did not speak. It was probably his imagination, but at this point, he wasn't going to dismiss anything. He listened again, hoping to hear the words again. But nothing came.

The baby started to move more, and this was not helping the situation. Images formed in his mind that he assumed his daughter sent him, telling him what he must do. This time he listened. He removed the swaddling from Amber and held her while Miriam started to cry. He showed the baby to the swarm of snakes. Then something miraculous happened.

Amber tilted her head as if she was

looking directly at the biggest snake, and continued to stare at it. She moved her head to the other side…the snake followed her move. Then, Amber reached out with one of her hands and made a baby like noise. The snake's head detached from its body. The other snakes started to move around, slithering closer to the baby and the group. Nikoli was getting scared, but he remained steadfast to what he saw in his mind. She did it again. His baby daughter was killing the snakes, one by one. As he watched her, her eyes turned from green to yellow. The birthmark on her neck began to glow a slight red color.

The tree became filled with more snakes. Nikoli continued to hold Amber upright and let the baby do her magic. He was amazed at what he was witnessing, and glanced back to Malakai and Miriam. They too seemed amazed and in wonderment.

***

Amber continued to stare at the snakes. The voices inside her were telling her what to do. She was listening to the oldest voice, that of Illyris.

Look at the snakes, child. Point your finger. We will do the rest. Child, you must do this to live.

She pointed at the snakes, one by one, as if this were a game. As the snakes moved closer, she just pointed and they died. But one snake that she pointed at didn't die. She looked at it harder and harder, but it still didn't die. The souls inside her felt her fear and lent her the strength. Suddenly, she started to grow. Amber was getting bigger in Nikoli's arms. Sensing her father's disbelief, she didn't move but allowed him to shift

95

as she grew. He put her down on the ground.

Looking at her mother and her imprinted friend, she simply smiled and turned her eyes up to her father, and smiled at him as well. Then, with conviction, she turned to the snakes, raised her hand to the dark sky, and pointed downward to them. All the snakes were set aflame and the tree was burned to a crisp. Once that was done, there was no spreading of fire to endanger this family. When she reached her arms up to Nikoli, he bent down and picked her up.

She spoke, but not in a child's voice. "I am the soul of the true queen Illyris. Take the child and continue. I will return her to the baby you know. Speed is a must."

***

Miriam was crying at what she'd witnessed, fearful now more than ever.

But she obeyed and the family continued. What was happening with her baby? Was she making the right choice by giving her away? What if she and Nikoli ran away and kept her? Tears flowed down her cheeks but she carried on.

***

Malakai urged the others to move forward. Recalling the words of the stranger, he knew cunning must be used, and they must travel fast. Obstacles would be in place to try and prevent them from continuing on the journey. He sensed that Miriam might be fearful and want to keep the baby. His responsibility was the protection of Amber, with every fiber in his being.

Urging the group to move on, he relieved Nikoli of carrying Amber, who was back to her infant size. They moved in silence, unsure of what to say to each other based on what they had witnessed. All Malakai knew was that this baby was his to protect as much as she was her parents' responsibility. This child was the one that the prophecy spoke of. He couldn't help but wonder what other prophecies spoke of the child.

After a few hours of silent walking, the sun began to rise. The day was going to be beautiful. Malakai gave his thanks again for the strength to continue this journey.

CHAPTER SEVEN
GOODBYES

After several days of walking, another obstacle presented itself for the group. Nikoli knew they were almost to the city, but there was now another delay. Vampires had managed to catch up with them, as it was now night. He poised himself, leaving Malakai to hold the baby.

As they had been walking before they were interrupted by the vampires, Miriam had shared details about her life prior to meeting him. Her magic. He questioned her about this because of the special abilities that Amber presented to them…the way she communicated, the scare with the snakes, and other little things.

He learned that Miriam knew powerful spells, and was trained not only in light magic but dark magic as well. Because it was in her blood, he knew that it was inside Amber too. But right now, he was faced with vampires.

"Give us the baby and no harm will come to you. You know the rules. Your kind serves us and always has."

"The baby is not going with you. She is to live and fulfill her destiny," Nikoli responded in a stern and strong voice. "She is my daughter, and under my protection according to the laws of the pack."

A female vampire moved stealthily to the side, hoping to be within reach of the baby. But from the corner of his eye Nikoli caught a glance of Miriam moving toward her.

"Lamia, morte nocte, dabit me in vitute control. Sanguis est, non sitis. Audite me potestatem noctis."

The vampires covered their ears and began to shriek. Falling to their knees, they bowed in submission to Miriam. Her hands were stretched out in front of her, palms facing outward. Nikoli continued to watch his love. This was her power. Her magic.

"Obsecro vos omnes servos meos ad deteriora justo. Servabis me nemo. Crastinum invenire puella alia via."

The vampires screamed again in terror, but had no choice but to obey. Nikoli noticed that Miriam was not speaking in her kind voice, but in a voice of power. Could this be the dark magic she was brought up in? He then noticed that the baby was also crying and the birthmark was glowing. This time it was glowing brighter than it had with the snakes. A light glow was also forming around Amber. He wondered if Miriam noticed or if she was too busy.

Malakai noticed, it seemed, because he gave the baby back to Nikoli. Holding her once more, Nikoli raised the child so that she could face the vampires and her mother.

Then the baby did the most amazing thing again. Her birthmark glowed stronger, her eyes turned from green to red. She pointed her little fingers at the vampires and they were cast on fire. She then looked at Miriam and her eyes turned back to green. She pointed and started to cry. Miriam's hands caught on fire.

Nikoli noticed that Malakai rushed to her side and tried to put out the fire. Miriam was in a daze but managed to shake it off.

"What happened?"

"Everything, love. Were you using your dark magic? You seemed to have a power we have never seen before. Is this what you were telling me?"

Miriam shook her head, saying she didn't remember anything.

Nikoli decided it was time to continue on the last leg of the journey. They had to find the building with the angel for Amber to be safe.

***

Finally they reached the city. It had been a long journey from their camp to here. Amber was thriving and loved being with them based on how she was always smiling. Malakai walked a little faster than the parents because he knew they needed time to say goodbye, and he wanted to find the building. His heart was also breaking, knowing that he would have to say goodbye to the little girl he was beginning to feel protective over, but in order for her to live, he knew this was the right thing to do.

Motioning for the family that a break period was needed, they sat down in a restaurant. They had enough money to order their meal and then some. The place was not crowded at all. In fact, only one waitress and one cook attended the restaurant. A few customers were scattered here and there, but eventually they all left while the group was eating.

"Little Amber, you are much more than you seem. One day, I hope that we will meet again, and I pledge my life to protect yours. Nikoli, do you have the letter ready for the orphanage or wherever we will take her?"

"Yes, Malakai. It is written, along with her necklace. Not to fear. I think the only thing to fear is that Miriam is not herself."

"I'm okay, Nikoli and Malakai. Just heartbroken. It is not easy for a mother to do, but I know I must. I also don't trust the magic I was born with. Help me after this, please."

Malakai took her hand and nodded. He looked at the baby once more and a single tear flowed down his cheek. He noticed that Amber looked directly at him and smiled. Her eyes shone with a light, or so he thought. He was going to miss her, but he didn't want the others to see his loss. He recalled the words of the stranger. He must be strong.

***

Nikoli was quiet while eating his meal. He looked occasionally at the baby and did not say a word. The baby looked at him and smiled. He felt as if she gave him a loving embrace with those eyes, like a daughter hugging her father. Nikoli was going to miss her greatly, but knew the sacrifice that had to be made. For the good of the prophecy, for the good of the world.

He broke the silence by saying, "Malakai, you must stay close to her. We cannot. Miriam can't be near her if the dark magic is pulling at her. Protect Amber. Will you do that?"

"Yes, Nikoli. I take it I am not returning to the camp with you both?"

"That is correct, Malakai. Do not come with us. You are the imprinted chosen one. You must protect her. Watch her grow and fulfill her destiny if you can."

Malakai looked at the baby and then back at Nikoli. He nodded, and Nikoli took that as a sign of commitment. Placing the baby on his lap, Nikoli bounced her just a little, and she cooed. She was a beautiful baby, full of power, love, and strength. Closing his eyes, he reached out to her quietly.

Show me, child, show me the past life you lived if you can. Please. Show me that what we must do is right in order to protect you.

The baby smiled and showed him images of Illyris, the wolves in captivity, her strength to defy the vampires. He also saw the world around her in flames. Then the images changed. He saw a beautiful young woman and an older version, it seemed, of Malakai. Though he was wearing sunglasses and his hair was pulled back, it still looked like him. This image, he knew, meant that she survived in the end. He only hoped that he could rescue Miriam from the dark magic, because she told him that she didn't like the dark magic. She wanted to be like her father, a prophet. A good person.

It was time. It was time to find the building. But before they could leave, Miriam had a spell.

**

Miriam's eyes became white as if the pupils floated to the back of her head. She began to speak. "The queen is the child with green eyes, a marking on her neck. She is destined to be strong. She will know hate, love, sadness, joy, and pride, all before she is chosen to fulfill her role. The child will grow, but her bloodlines combine the past, the present, and future of all races. She is a child of the wolves, a human, a child of magic, a child of the seers. She will also become a child of the vampires. She will possess all the races, and will lead them all to unification. The child must live and grow to fulfill her destiny. Inside her is the soul of Illyris, the fated queen of the vampires, sentenced to rebirth in order to fulfill her destiny. Inside her is also the marking of the Dark Man. She will have enemies, she will have friends. But, for now, she must live."

Miriam leaned forward and looked at her husband and Malakai. They looked back at her, because she'd just told them the things that they feared for the baby. This one special child was a child of the prophecy, who would one day become queen of the prophecy. The one the ages foretold of.

"It is time. We must go. Let me take the baby and say goodbye. Her life must start now."

Miriam clutched the baby tightly. It was as if Amber sensed the goodbye, because she sent her mother an image of love. Miriam knew her baby would be okay.

They walked around the town till they found the building with the angel. Having a mother's courage, she placed the amulet around Amber's neck, kissed her, and rang the bell.

A lady answered. Miriam said the words. "To save my baby, I must give her to you. Keep her safe."

The lady looked at the party and back at the baby. Glancing around, she ushered them inside quickly. Miriam and the men were guided into the office, where they listened to the woman talk about the orphanage. Noticing her trinkets on the desk and shelves, Miriam noticed one that caught her eye. She remembered her father having one as well. It was a sign of the order. She decided to break the conversation.

"Do you know Talios?"

The lady stopped and stared at her with a questionable look. "Yes, I know Talios. He is a great seer, if you believe in that sort of thing."

"Yes I do. Do you know of his daughter?"

"I recall that he had a daughter, but she has been long gone for many years. He doesn't talk about it since he failed to get his little girl back. You must know our order to know him by name. It isn't something we discuss publicly. Who are you?"

Miriam gathered her courage and realized this was going to sound crazy. "I am Miriam, daughter to Talios. I have both dark magic and his gifts inside me.

I was raised in dark magic since I was taken. And this is my baby. Do you know of the prophecy?"

The woman stood up and pressed a button. Miriam knew she must have sounded like a fruitcake to this woman. But she continued.

"My daughter is Amber. She needs protection now. I can't guard her with dark magic, and I have not seen my father since I was five. She is the one the prophecy speaks of. All races will come through her bloodline now and in the future. Do you understand what I'm telling you? There is no one else for me to turn to."

Before she could receive an answer, the door opened. An elderly man stood before them. He looked healthy but he also looked broken.

The woman spoke. "Talios, this is

Miriam and her family. Do you remember Miriam? Do you know the name of your daughter?"

Talios looked at Miriam and the baby. He spoke.

"The heavens sent you to me. I am not strong as I once was, but I used the strongest power I could have. Did the guide tell you to come north? To me here?"

Miriam nodded. "Malakai received the message. That's him over there. But I thought you were dead. And you are here, in front of me. I do not understand."

***

Talios smiled. "Then it worked. My death was a ruse made in hopes to find my daughter again and to keep her safe. I'm terribly sorry for the pain it might have caused, but it needed to be done. I needed the power of the white light and her mother, bless her heart, was full of dark light." He smiled and then said, "I lost my daughter a long time ago to the Dark Man. I am a seer, but I also have light magic. That means my daughter has light magic as well. My daughter would be a powerful seer if she had not been taken. But alas, that's not why you are here today. Your baby, you claim, is the queen. Let me see the baby."

He looked at the baby, staring into her eyes, and the little one stared back at him. He matched his eyes to hers as if they were communicating. Then Talios smiled and said, "She is the one. She is saved."

Then, he looked back at the woman who claimed to be his daughter. He stared into her eyes, and his eyes filled with tears.

"You are her. You are my daughter.

The order has found the missing daughter! Mrs. Beasley, tell the others. She has returned."

Talios was not strong. He told the others he must rest, but would return in a while. His daughter had returned, found her way from darkness to light. And the future of the child and the races now had a chance to be saved.

Chapter Eight
Future

Amber was placed in the orphanage and seemed happy. Nikoli and Miriam stayed on for a few days to reunite with her father. Malakai parted, but found housing in the city so he could protect Amber when needed. Nikoli loved Miriam with all his heart, but he sensed that the revelation of finding her father played with her heart. Not to mention she was losing her baby. It was not the time to say that they could always have another.

Bringing her breakfast on the final

day that they were there, Nikoli wanted to know what they were going to do.

"Love, what do you want to do? Do you wish to stay with your father, or do you want to return home with me? Tell me."

Miriam looked at him and smiled lovingly. "I will go with you, husband, where you go."

Nikoli kissed her on the forehead and fed her by his own hand. "We will leave once you say goodbye to Talios. We will have a long journey. But first, are you sure?"

"Yes, husband. I am sure. I need to know how to conquer the dark magic. I don't want to be part of the side that wants to kill our daughter. Let me go see my father."

***

Talios was in his small apartment

when he heard the knock on the door. He knew it would be Miriam. He hoped she would stay, but he knew that would be harder on her having given up her baby.

"Talios...er, I mean Father...I choose to leave with Nikoli. We have a future with his pack. But I want to know from you, can I remove this dark magic that is inside me?"

Talios put down the paper and took a sip of his coffee. "Daughter, it is hard to remove something that is inside you. You will need powerful magic to overcome the Dark Man's evil work. But there is a way. I'm afraid I'm not that strong anymore, but if you choose the path, your husband will need to continue home without you. You will need to go to the order and seek counsel to their ways. You will need to sacrifice the life with Nikoli to be a child of the order once more. Is that your wish?"

Miriam cried. She couldn't think about leaving her love. It was already hard that they were losing their baby to save her. She knew Nikoli would not survive if she abandoned him too. Silently, she shook her head no. With tears in her eyes and her voice trembling, she quietly said, "My place is with my husband. I will live with the dark and the light inside me, as well as the fact that I had to save Amber. We leave immediately. Goodbye, Father. Promise me, protect the future queen."

Talios promised and knew he would never see his child again. But he had his granddaughter here until a family took her in. He only hoped that her future would save them all.

After Miriam and Nikoli left, he looked in on the baby. He smiled at Amber and she smiled back knowingly about what her future held.

After all, he knew she would be queen.

An Excerpt from Blood Prophecy Three: Queen's Ascension

Elizabeth Southern (Owd Demdike), England 1564

Elizabeth Southern was a woman of piety until the day she met a young boy named Tibet. She found him sitting at the edge of the dirt road, looking hungry, scared, and alone. Hoisting up her skirts a little, she knelt by the boy.

"What is thy name, child?" As she asked him, she reached into her satchel and pulled out a piece of day old bread.

Looking up at her with his dark brown eyes, he didn't smile or anything, just grabbed the bread from her fingers and tore into it hungrily. Crumbs fell from his mouth down to his dirty shirt.

"Tibet," he said with his mouth full. "But ye will know me as many names, thy mother."

"I know not what you sayeth. I am a God-fearing woman. I do not speak filth."

Elizabeth was ready to move on because her faith prevented her from wanting to stay, but she found that her feet would not walk away. The boy rose and stood in front of her. She was scared. Holding her hands together, Elizabeth began to pray for salvation. Inside she felt that this was the devil's work at hand.

The boy looked up at her and before she could scream, he changed to a black cow. The cow stood before her and stared into her soul. Suddenly, Elizabeth heard a voice in her mind, commanding her to undress. Failing to resist, she removed her skirts and shift, letting them fall to the road. In modesty she used her hands to cover herself.

"Thy mother will not cover herself," she heard the voice say. It was the same sound as the boy's voice.

"Thy mother will head the family of witches. From thy line, a dark path will be born. Ye will practice from the man that will visit. Similar visits will be made to thy children, relatives, neighbors. To conjure the destruction of light, ye will lead the dark. I will guide thee till thou is dead."

The animal then transformed to the version of a man. He stood there naked and ready.

"Ye shall not sign thy name to my book, but instead will take my seed and give birth to the next."

Before she could resist the man covered her with his body, and when the deed was done, she remained naked and alone in the middle of the dirt road. Her virtuous behavior was no more.

Many years later, Elizabeth found her home occupied with her children and grandchildren, each one different but strong in the practice. Looking back on the day she met Tibet, she also wondered when he would return. Her questions were answered when Alizon came home talking about meeting a boy who could change into a dog, and how she felt happy to help him whenever he needed it by becoming a witch. Elizabeth knew that the devil's work was at hand.

Elizabeth Bathory, Hungary 1600

Elizabeth couldn't stand living with her husband Ferenc Nádasdy any longer. Having been engaged to him since she was ten, she grew out of love with the man and held nothing but contempt. In secrecy, she needed to perform her rituals, and it was getting harder and harder. She began to poison his food little by little.

One night, she invited one of the young maidens from the village to dine with her. Ferenc was feeling ill; in fact, he'd begun to lose the use of his legs. This was perfect. Elizabeth dined with the young girl, laughing and talking over a finely cooked meal.

"Young woman, did you enjoy the meal?"

"Oh, yes, mistress. It was exquisite and fine. I loved the wine especially," she said while giggling.

"Ah, the wine. It's my own making, this wine." Elizabeth smiled and decided it was time to head towards her special room.

Guiding the young maid, who was still giggling, towards the room, Elizabeth hurried the young woman in. Being careful to not let the servants hear them, she looked the girl in the eyes.

"You want to sleep. Go to sleep now." The young girl fell to the floor and began to snore. Stepping around her, Elizabeth knelt down and shifted the young girl as if she was cradling her. Moving her hair, she decided to bite into the neck. Blood poured out, covering the bare neck and dripping down her bodice. Elizabeth reached into the blood and covered her hands in it. Then she licked her fingers and wash them once more in the blood. Moving her hands towards her face, she began to bathe in the blood. In Elizabeth's mind, she was doing this to stay young.

The door to the room opened and the noise startled Elizabeth. A man stood in the doorway, his hat tipped low, hiding his face. In fact, it looked like he didn't have a face at all, but only two eyes leering out at Elizabeth.

He spoke, but only in her mind. *Thy mother, the blood will renew you, but you need the blood of a queen, not a waif. Seek the queen, find her blood, and bathe in its glory. In return, I will keep you young for all time.*

Then he disappeared. Elizabeth returned to the bathing in blood but realized that this was not the queen. She decided to discard the body by cutting it into pieces and boiling it in the kitchen. It was time to make a soup for the morrow's meal.

Having been born and raised in Hawaii, I loved telling stories ever since I was a child about vampires, werewolves, angels, demons, and witches. I was a little girl who loved scary stories, much to my mother's dismay. The scarier - the better. Hawaii was a perfect place for stories until I moved to Seattle. I decided to turn a love for the supernatural into writing stories to see if others would love them as much as I do. Currently, I live in Florida but since I'm a Seattle girl at heart, my stories take place in the Northwest. I continue to write supernatural stories of vampires, werewolves, witches, and more while enjoying the beaches and sunshine.

Amber: The Birth of a Queen

Barb Jones

AMBER: THE BIRTH OF A QUEEN

Amber: The Birth of a Queen

BARB JONES

Amber: The Birth of a Queen

BARB JONES

AMBER: THE BIRTH OF A QUEEN

BARB JONES

Amber: The Birth of a Queen

Amber: The Birth of a Queen

AMBER: THE BIRTH OF A QUEEN

Barb Jones

Amber: The Birth of a Queen

BARB JONES